THE USBORNE BOOK Of
PAPIER MACHE

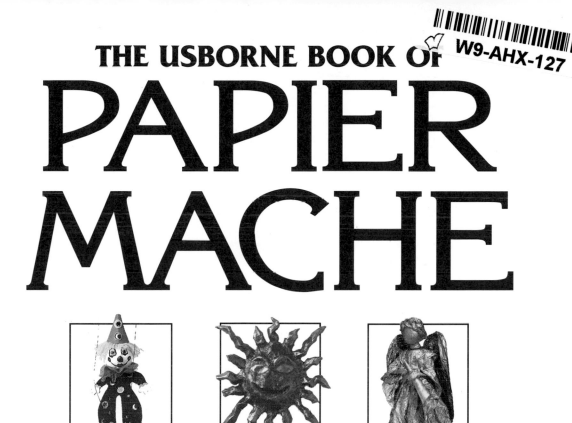

Ray Gibson

Edited by Cheryl Evans with Fiona Watt

Designed by Robert Walster and Jane Felstead

Photographs by Amanda Heywood • Illustrated by Prue Greener
Series editor: Cheryl Evans

Contents

Before you start	2	Tray	18
Surprise fruit	4	Egg holder duck	20
Bangles and beads	6	Monster mask	22
Starry bowl	8	Christmas angel	24
Mirror frames	10	Puppets	27
Tiger plate	12	Lizard planter	30
Rabbit family	14	Recipes	32
Monster's foot pencil holder	16		

First published in 1995. Usborne Publishing Ltd., Usborne House, 83-85 Saffron Hill, London EC1N 8RT, England.
Copyright ©1995 Usborne Publishing Ltd. First published in America August 1995.

Before you start

Papier mâché, pronounced pap-ee-yay mashay, is a French phrase, meaning "chewed paper". You make it from old newspapers and paste. There are two main ways to use papier mâché: pasted in layers or as a pulp mixed with paste. There are recipes for the paste and how to mix the pulp on page 32. Which method to use is explained for each project.

Most papier mâché projects are not hard, but they can take a while to finish, as you must allow lots of time for the layers or wet pulp to dry. It's best to make things in stages over several days.

Layering

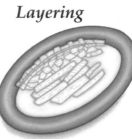

Use small pieces of paper over curved parts.

Use paper strips on flat areas.

Layering means pasting layers of small pieces of paper over a base shape. When it is dry, you usually remove the base, although sometimes it is left in place. What you get is a strong, light papier mâché shell, the shape of the base.

Tips on layering

1. Cut or tear paper into strips. Torn edges give a smoother finish.

2. Brush paste on lots of pieces at once on a tray, with a big paintbrush.

3. Smooth overlapping pieces of pasted paper onto the base shape with your fingers.

4. Complete one layer at a time. You will be told how many layers to do each time.

Pulp

Pulp is wet newspaper mashed with paste and glue until it feels like soft clay. You can use it to create solid shapes and model it with your fingers or tools. It is used in thin layers, dried each time. Thick layers may dry on the outside, but seal in moisture which can make it rot.

Tips on using pulp

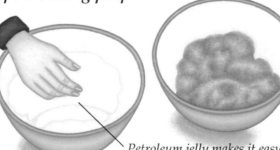

Petroleum jelly makes it easy to pull the shell off the base.

1. If you are using a base shape, smear it with petroleum jelly first.

2. Roll and flatten small balls of pulp in your hands. Press all over the surface.

3. Make sure there are no gaps. Smooth the places where balls join with your fingers.

Drying

Let projects dry naturally in an even heat. If you put them next to direct heat, they can dry unevenly and warp. Place them on plastic foodwrap on a flat surface.

Papier mâché never looks exciting before it is decorated. (See page 20 for a finished duck.)

You can try different kinds of paper, but not shiny magazine paper (the paste won't soak in).

These shapes are primed with water and glue mixed.

Priming

Priming means to prepare for decorating. You prime with white emulsion paint under pale shades, or a mix of two parts PVA (household) glue to one part water under dark shades.

This box is primed with white emulsion.

Painting

Use acrylic or poster paints. If you use poster paints, mix a little PVA (household) glue in with them. If you don't, they may smear when you varnish (see below).

Polyurethane varnish

Small decorator's brush

Paintbrush

Varnishing

Varnish gives a shiny top layer that makes things look rich and glowing. You can make a simple varnish to use (see page 8) or buy polyurethane varnish. Ask an adult to help you use this, as it has poisonous fumes.

Acrylic paints

These things have been fully painted and varnished.

3

Surprise fruit

You will need: fruit or vegetables as base shapes; one quantity of paste (page 32); old newspapers; petroleum jelly; craft knife; white emulsion paint; decorator's brush; rice, pasta or dried lentils; poster paints mixed with PVA (household) glue, or acrylic paints; paintbrush.

Keep smoothing the pasted paper with your fingers.

1. Use any firm fruit or vegetables such as apples, pears, lemons, red peppers. Rub them all over with petroleum jelly.

2. Cut or tear 2cm (1in) squares of newspaper and paste over the fruit. If they will not lie flat, tear them a little smaller.

3. Allow it to dry. Do three more layers, drying completely between each one. Dry naturally in a warm, airy place.

Tips

Paint the background first and allow to dry before you decorate. It is easier to put dark shades on top of pale ones.

You could paint the fruit to look real, like the peppers and chillies in the picture. Look closely at the real thing and copy it.

For a fruit that jingles, put in a toy bell at step 5. You can buy bells from craft or department stores.

You can see how to make bowls like these on pages 8-9.

Maracas are musical instruments. Shake them rhythmically to make a rattling noise in time to music.

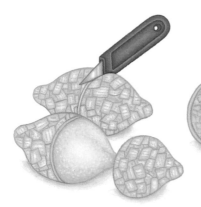

Stand to dry on unpainted part.

4. Ask someone to help you cut around the middle of the shape with a craft knife. Ease the paper shape off the fruit.

5. In one half of your paper shape, put a few grains of rice, some pasta shapes or lentils. Replace the other half to match exactly.

6. Paste paper strips in all directions over where the halves join. Leave to dry. Paint with white emulsion, one side at a time.

7. When it is completely dry, paint any designs you like on it. Look at the photograph below for some ideas.

Maracas

Make two orange shapes, as in the steps above. Before you paint them, add long handles, like this.

You need: two slim cardboard rolls; scissors; clear tape; newspaper.

Cut two rolls to about 10cm (4in) long. You could cut both from a long kitchen roll tube.

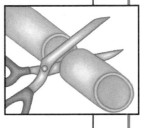

Stuff newspaper in one end. Tape other end to the orange shape and cover with paper strips.

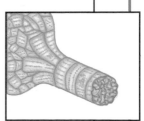

5

Bangles and beads

You will need: one quantity of paper pulp (page 32); thin cardboard, such as a cereal box; silver foil; acrylic or poster paints; paintbrush; PVA (household) glue; soft cloth; scissors; fastenings (see right).

These steps show how to make base shapes. See how to turn them into things to wear on the right.

1. Cut a shape from thin cardboard. Press a small ball of pulp, onto the middle of it and ease out to the edges in a thin layer.

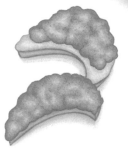

2. Leave to dry naturally (up to a day). Add more pulp on top, squeezing and pressing it into a rounded-out shape.

For a jewel box, sandpaper a small box, cover with paper layers then create a pulp design on lid.

Brooches made using silver foil.

3. Leave to dry again. Add more layers if you want it bigger, or decorate with small beads or rolls of pulp for raised patterns.

4. When dry, tear a piece of silver foil twice the size of your shape. Spread glue all over the shape.

You can simply prime your shape, then paint it, if you like

These beads are brightly painted.

5. Press the shiny side of the foil onto the glue. Smooth it all over with a soft cloth, starting from the middle.

6. Turn the shape over and trim the foil to 0.5cm (¼in). Glue the back, then press the foil edge down onto it neatly.

Paint stays in wrinkles.

7. Paint over the foil front. Wait a moment, then wipe most of the paint off with a damp cloth. Repeat until you like the effect. For other effects, see the photograph.

All these things are very light to wear.

Brooch

Choker with silver foil

Clip earrings

For pierced earrings, make a hole with a needle to slip hooks through (buy hooks from craft stores).

These earrings are brushed with gold acrylic paint.

Make bangles any width you like. Add pulp shapes to make them more interesting.

Slip beads onto strong thread and tie for a necklace.

Making things to wear: Earrings

To make earrings match, turn a shape over, draw around it and cut out again before adding pulp. Glue on earring clips (from craft stores).

Choker

Cut a short length of drinking straw. Tape it to the back of your shape. Thread a shoelace through it to tie around your neck.

Brooch

Attach a safety pin to the back with strong tape.

More ways to make things: Beads

Flatten a small lump of pulp, fold it around a short length of drinking straw and shape into a bead. Make sure the straw doesn't show. Slip the bead onto a paintbrush to finish shaping, if you like. Paint when dry.

Bracelet

Overlap and tape a thin cardboard strip into a circle that will slide onto your wrist. Slip it over a bottle to hold while you add a layer of pulp and extra shapes. Decorate brightly.

Starry bowl

You will need:

1½ -2 quantities of pulp and extra paste (page 32); bowl; petroleum jelly; paper towels; a big potato; sharp knife; blunt knife; gold and blue paint (poster paint with glue, or acrylic); blue tissue paper; PVA (household) glue; scissors; paintbrush; felt tip pen; saucer.

1. Choose a bowl to use as a base (a big one's best for this design). Smear the inside with a layer of petroleum jelly.

2. Take walnut-sized dollops of pulp, roll them in your palms, then flatten between your hands to about 4mm (¼in) thick.

3. Press flattened pulp all over the bowl. Start from the bottom and work up the sides. Smooth it as you go with your fingers.

The small bowl has a droopy rim made from pulp.

You can invent all kinds of designs for bowls.

Varnishing

Varnish is a clear coating to protect the surface and make it shiny.

To varnish, paint all over with PVA (household) glue mixed with a little water. It looks cloudy but dries clear.

Allow to dry. Do more layers for a harder, shinier finish. You can wipe it clean with a damp cloth.

Paste

4. Keep smoothing over the joins. At the end, dip your fingers in paste and smooth all over. Leave the top edge wavy.

5. Leave the bowl to dry naturally in an even heat. This may take up to four days so be patient. You can feel when it is dry.

6. When completely dry, run an old, blunt knife between the original bowl and the pulp. Ease the pulp bowl out.

7. Carefully wipe all the petroleum jelly off the pulp bowl with a paper towel, otherwise the paint will not stick to it.

8. To prime it, paint all over with 1 part water to 2 parts PVA (household) glue. Now it is ready to decorate (see right).

For this bowl, add pulp lumps once it is dry. Then paint.

Decorating the bowl

Be very careful with sharp knives.

Don't worry if star prints look patchy.

Smooth stars on by brushing with more glue mix.

1. Paint the inside gold. When dry, paint the outside blue. Take care not to go over the rim, where the paints meet.

2. Cut the potato in half. Draw on a star with felt-tip pen. Cut away a layer of potato around the star. Dry on a paper towel.

3. Put gold paint onto a saucer and press the potato star into it. Print several times onto the tissue. Allow to dry.

4. Cut the stars out roughly. Spread glue and water mixed onto the outside of the bowl and glue stars on. Varnish (see left).

9

Mirror frames

You will need: a small mirror; strong cardboard; pencil; ruler; craft knife; newspaper; one quantity runny paste (page 32); plastic tray; small decorator's brush; masking tape; strong string; tissue paper; white emulsion paint; poster or acrylic paints; PVA (household) glue.

1. Place your mirror in the middle of the cardboard and draw around it. Draw a second line 0.5cm (¼in) inside the first.

2. Cut out the inside shape, using a craft knife and a ruler. You can draw and cut out other inner shapes, if you want (see below).

3. Draw a frame of any size and shape you like around the hole. Draw around cups, plates or food cans for curves. Cut out the shape.

4. Lay newspaper strips about 4 x 7cm (1¾ x 2¾in) on the tray and brush them all with paste. Use the decorator's brush.

5. Paste strips, overlapping, all over one side of the frame. This will be the front. Paste strips over the edge, all around. Dry.

Dry each layer.

6. Do three more layers. For a smooth finish, add a layer of tissue paper. Do one layer of paper strips on the frame's back.

7. When dry, paint the front white. Dry again, then do the back. When dry, decorate it. Put the mirror in the frame (see right).

Other ideas

Draw around a cup, saucer or plate to make a round hole and cut it out. Or do a freehand shape.

Oval inside shape.

Cut the outside frame into a fish, dinosaur or other animal. Paint it brightly, or do realistic markings.

Tape the shapes together, then join with pasted strips over the edges.

Tape mirror to show through hole.

Cut two hand mirror shapes, with a hole in one. Cover both with strips. Tape mirror between and join the shapes. Decorate.

You can use bright ribbons to hang your mirrors instead of string.

Attach ribbons very firmly with lots of strong tape.

You can hold this dinosaur by its tail as a hand mirror.

Paint a pretty hand mirror pink and gold.

Pasting strips around corners

To cover corners neatly, paste a strip across the corner, to hang over the edge.

Tear the overhanging part in half longways up as far as the edge of the frame.

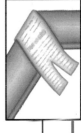

Bend and stick each half down separately onto the back of the frame.

Framing

Turn frame face-down. Tape the mirror face-down over the hole with masking tape.

Knot the ends of a short piece of string and attach to the back with lots more tape.

11

Tiger plate

You will need: a flat, oval plate as a base; one quantity of paste and one of pulp (see page 32); newspaper strips; PVA (household) glue; white emulsion paint; small decorating paintbrush; petroleum jelly; scissors; poster or acrylic paints; felt-tip pen; white tissue paper; kitchen paper.

This dish has a pulp snake protecting its eggs.

1. Smear the plate with a thin layer of petroleum jelly on your fingers. Don't leave any bare parts.

Let strips stick over the edge.

2. Paste a layer of strips across the plate (see page 2 for tips on this). Use shorter strips on curved parts.

3. Smooth paste on the first layer with your fingers and paste a second layer the other way. Dry (about 1 day).

Paint the back of the plate, too.

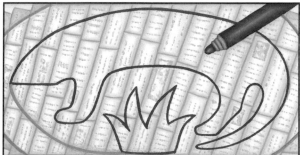

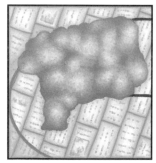

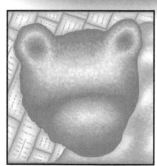

4. Repeat steps 2 and 3. When the plate is dry again, do the same twice more (eight layers in all). Draw a tiger's body and a tropical plant like this with felt-tip pen. Use the curve of the plate for the tiger's back.

5. Roll and flatten balls of pulp within the outline to make a raised shape (see page 2 for help with pulp).

6. When dry (2 days) build up a head. Do a round pulp shape and add a small lump for a chin and round ears.

Use a round plate for a cat with an arched back.

This plate has a checked tablecloth background with a lobster on it.

A plate takes 9 or 10 days to finish as it needs time to dry at each stage.

Don't take the paper off too soon, it will buckle.

Tissue paper makes it smoother.

7. When completely dry (about 2 more days), ease the paper off the dish. Trim the edge with scissors.

8. Wipe off all the petroleum jelly with kitchen paper. Glue strips over the edges. Dry (a few hours).

9. Paste on two layers of torn tissue paper. When dry (an hour or two) paint white, one side at a time.

10. Paint the main blocks, dry, then add patterns. Do two coats of PVA (household) glue varnish (page 8).

Rabbit family

You will need: one egg per rabbit; darning needle; saucer; pulp, not too wet - one quantity makes about four rabbits; PVA (household) glue; white emulsion paint; paints; white tissue paper; plastic food wrap; masking tape; plate; paintbrush; pencil. They take about four days.

Making the body

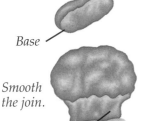

Base

Smooth the join.

Base added to flattened side of egg.

1. Blow one egg (see below) for each rabbit body. If you find it too hard, ask an adult to help. Rinse the shell in water and dry it.

2. Press marble-sized balls of pulp into a thin coat all over the egg. Roll and smooth the egg in your palms, then press it, on its side, onto food wrap.

3. Roll and flatten a slightly bigger ball of pulp. Press it onto the body and shape into a flat base, as shown. Allow it to dry (one or two days).

Blowing an egg

1. Gently wash and dry an egg. Pierce a hole in the blunt end with the needle. Wiggle the needle around to enlarge the hole.

Put tape on before making the hole to prevent cracking.

Shape and paint carrots and lettuce leaves for your rabbits from pulp.

2. Hold the end with the hole in it over the saucer. Pierce the other end. Wiggle the needle vigorously to break up the egg yolk.

3. Blow very hard through the top hole until everything inside is pushed out. It is really hard to start with, but it gets easier.

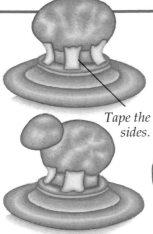

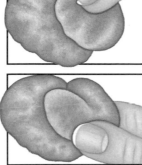

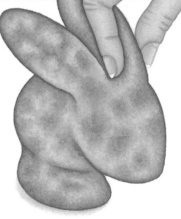

Tape the sides.

Smooth the joins.

4. Attach the base to an overturned plate with tape. Roll and flatten a walnut-sized ball of pulp. Press to the pointed end of the body for a head.

5. Shape the head into a heart like this: press a dip in the top with a finger; pinch the bottom into a point. The sides taper down in a curve.

6. Roll two fat pulp sausage shapes for ears. Lay them side by side along the rabbit's back. Join each to one of the bumps on the head.

7. Pinch a ridge along the top edges of the ears. Keep shaping the head and ears until they look right. Add a round tail. Let it dry (one day).

These rabbits are painted quite realistically; but you could do a family with bright patterns on.

Decoration

Tail

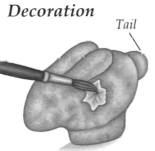

Cover a walnut in the same way for a baby rabbit.

1. Glue the rabbit, then press tiny pieces of white tissue paper all over it. Push paper into nooks and folds with a paintbrush.

2. Add a second layer when dry (an hour or less). The tissue layers give a smoother finish. Prime it (see page 3). Now paint as you like.

Features

Mark where the eyes will go in pencil first to make sure they are level.

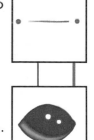

Paint the eyes brown and black as shown. Add white dots for glints.

Do a heart-shaped nose, a mouth, and streaks for whiskers.

Show where the back legs are with a thin black streak on the side.

Monster's foot pencil holder

You need: a clean, empty food can (400g/14oz); pencil; thin cardboard; newspaper; scissors; masking tape; PVA (household) glue; tissue paper; acrylic paints and brush; paste and 1½-2 quantities of pulp (page 32); old, blunt knife. **Tip:** make the foot on a tray, so you can move it without disturbing it.

1. Cut several strips of newspaper about 2 x 4cm (¾ x 1¾in). Paste them around the open edge of the food can, overlapping.

2. Place the can on the cardboard, near one edge, and draw around it. This will be the heel part of the monster's foot.

3. Draw around the heel and out in front of the can to make a big foot shape with three toes, spaced well apart. Cut it out.

4. Tape the tin onto its circle with masking tape. Fold a newspaper package to fit on the front of the foot. Tape it on.

5. Make newspaper rolls to fit inside each toe shape. Tape them on. Press flattened balls of pulp all over the can and foot.

6. Smooth the pulp with your fingers - do between the toes with the knife. Add a second layer, leaving a ragged top edge.

7. Roll and pinch balls of pulp and place them up the heel as spines. Press and pinch small balls on all over for bumpy skin.

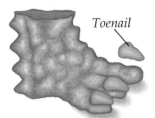

Toenail

8. Press and shape rough triangles for toenails and press onto the toes. Add more layers to make them thicker.

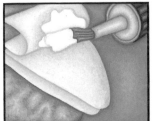

9. When the nails are dry, paste on three layers of tissue paper for a smoother finish. Leave to dry properly (up to 4 days).

10. Make more pulp if you need to. Press a thin layer all over the sole. Leave to dry. Prime, then paint inside and out.

Make monster pencil ends by shaping lumps of pulp around the pencil. Stand in a pot to dry, then paint.

Gruesome hand

Use the same technique for this gruesome hand.

Paste strips around the top of the can, as shown in step 1 of the monster foot.

Cover the can with pulp and build up a hand with three fingers around the side.

Add long nails to the fingers, as in steps 8 and 9 of the monster foot. Paint brightly.

Varnish the foot (page 8) if you want it to be shiny.

Do contrasting bumps.

Red and black make a strong combination.

You may need to paint two layers inside.

Tray

You will need: a small, round tray; newspapers; runny paste (page 32 - make one quantity, then more if needed); small decorator's paintbrush; gift wrap; scissors; PVA (household) glue; plastic food wrap.

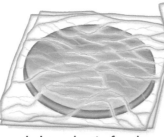

1. Lay plastic food wrap on a table. Turn the tray over onto it. Cover the tray with more food wrap.

2. Cut a piece of newspaper big enough to cover the whole tray and down its sides completely.

3. Use this as a guide to cut 17 more sheets. Protect a surface to work on. Lay one of the cut sheets on top.

Varnish (see page 8) for a shiny, wipeable surface.

This project is quite quick to make, but needs a few days to dry and finish, so allow for this if making a present.

4. Paste over it and lay a second piece on top. Smooth flat with your hands. Repeat with all the cut sheets.

5. Lift all 18 layers of paper and lay them over the tray. With paste on your fingers, smooth it down well.

6. Press the paper over the edges and down the sides. Smooth down any folds as flat as you can.

7. Press and smooth until satisfied. Allow to dry a little. When edges are bendy, like leather, trim to shape.

Paste strips over top edge.

8. Once the paper is very hard and dry (up to three days), lift off. Unpeel the food wrap. It will be damp below.

9. Leave to dry. If the tray starts to bend, keep it flat with food cans. Neaten the edge with paper strips.

To decorate

1. Cut some big motifs from the gift wrap. Cut the background into small pieces. Don't tear it or white edges will show.

2. Dip background pieces in paste and glue all over the tray, overlapping. Dry. Arrange the big motifs, then glue on with as little paste as possible.

Personalized tray

Make a very special present by personalizing a tray. Paste on a picture of the person and surround it by images of things she likes.

Cut out and glue on letters from a magazine for her name.

Nina likes animals, food, music and parties with her friends.

Egg holder duck

You will need:

two cardboard rolls; kitchen roll; one quantity of paste (page 32); newspaper; masking tape; box 11 x 16cm (4 x 6½in) and 8cm (3in) deep*; ruler; pencil; two plastic toy eyes (from craft stores); scissors; white emulsion paint; paints; decorator's brush; PVA (household) glue.

Basic shape

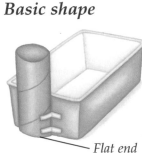

Flat end

1. Flatten one end of a 15cm (6in) length of cardboard roll. Tape it firmly to the middle of one end of the box.

Look at photograph to judge size of head.

2. Crumple up a sheet of newspaper 40 x 60cm (15½ x 22in). Wrap in the sheet of kitchen roll and tape.

3. Shape the parcel into an oval head. Squeeze it tighter if it looks too big. Tape to the top of the neck.

Torn tissue paper strips were added to this duck, for extra, glowing depth.

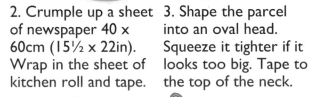

2cm (¾in)

Cut V shape

Round off like this.

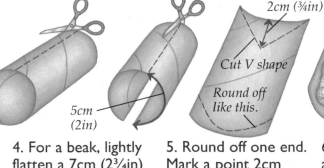

5cm (2in)

4. For a beak, lightly flatten a 7cm (2¾in) length of cardboard roll. Cut along it. Cut again 5cm (2in) from the first cut.

5. Round off one end. Mark a point 2cm (¾in) in from the middle of the other end. Cut from each corner to this point.

6. Flatten the beak and trim rounded end to a neat shape. Bend back into a curve. Pad with crumpled paper. Tape to hold in place.

7. Press the V-shape onto the front of the head and tape it securely. Don't worry if it looks a little bit messy at this stage.

Finishing the shape

Fold long sides together.

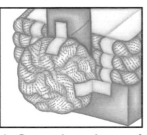

1. Fold a piece of newspaper 38 x 28cm (15 x 11in). Fold again and twist. Trim to 30cm (12in). Make 6 altogether.

Gap

2. Tape one twist around the rim of the box, starting at the neck. Tape one on the other side and join them into a tail.

Add tape across here.

3. Tape on the other twists. Bend them up at the tail and tape to the top twist. Crumple newspaper to fill the gap. Tape to hold.

4. Crumple a sheet of newspaper into a pad. Tape it to the box, over the neck roll. Flatten the pad's edges against the box.

Paste paper inside and out.

5. Using the layering method (see page 2) paste on four layers of newspaper. Paste over gaps to smooth shapes together.

6. Leave in a warm, airy place to dry out completely (1-2 days). Paint all over with white emulsion and leave to dry.

You can keep eggs to eat in the duck or decorate blown (see page 14) or hard boiled eggs for an attractive display.

These eggs were painted white first, pasted with tissue squares, then decorated with gold acrylic paint and 3-D pen (from art suppliers).

Varnish (page 8) eggs to make them shine.

Eyes

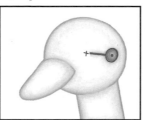

1. Mark a dot for each eye. Poke in a pencil to make a hole. Glue the prong on each toy eye and press into the holes.

To decorate

Decorate your duck as you like. Paint it with poster paints and glue, or acrylics; you can then paste on layers of overlapping green, blue, yellow and mauve tissue paper for a richer look, as in the photograph, if you like. Varnish (page 8) for a shiny finish.

Monster mask

You will need: plain flour, salt, cooking oil for saltdough (see below); silver foil; big tray; saucer; plastic food wrap; newspaper; white tissue paper; 1½-2 quantities paste (page 32); paintbrush; pencil; petroleum jelly; craft knife; blunt knife; scissors; poster or acrylic paints; thin hat elastic.

The dough shape

1. To get a pattern for the basic shape, press foil lightly onto your face. Quickly scratch holes for your nostrils.

2. Now press the foil firmly all over your face, right to the edges. Lift off and trim the face shape.

3. Place the saucer upside down on the tray. Cover both with plastic food wrap. Make the saltdough.

4. Roll and flatten a big ball of dough over the saucer to roughly the size and shape of your foil pattern.

5. Place the foil onto the dough. Press where your eyes are on the foil to make dents in the dough.

6. Add the monster's features in dough as shown below. The shapes to add are shown dark green.

To make saltdough

1. Mix together four mugs of plain flour, two mugs of salt, one tablespoon of cooking oil.

2. Add enough water to make it cling together as a stiff dough. Knead it thoroughly with your fingers.

① *Big rolls above and below eyes.*

Frown marks

Huge, triangular nose (your nose will fit inside)

Lumps for upper lip and chin

② *Curved horns*

Round ears

Cheekbones

Press red areas with a finger to mark nostrils, ears and upper lip.

Pointed fangs

Lower lip

Making the mask

Paste on small squares

Use a craft knife.

Slip a hand under mask to pull dough out of hollows.

Add a tissue paper layer for a smooth finish.

1. After about a day and a half, the dough's surface will be hard. Smear with petroleum jelly and paste on five layers of newspaper.

2. When dry (allow a day), ease the mask off the dough shape. Run a blunt knife under the edges to loosen. Dry again.

3. Trim the edge of the mask to neaten. Cut out the nostrils and eye shapes. Paste overlapping paper strips over all edges.

4. When dry, poke holes in the ears with a pencil. Tie on elastic from ear to ear, long enough to stretch around your head.

Paint the mask as you like. This one is dark green with lighter green markings and fiery orange touches.

To age the mask, brush all over with watery black paint.

More shapes

Use the saltdough to make other shapes for papier mâché objects. This sun wall plaque was also shaped around an upturned saucer.

Shape long, wobbly "rays" and press in eye and mouth dents.

Christmas angel

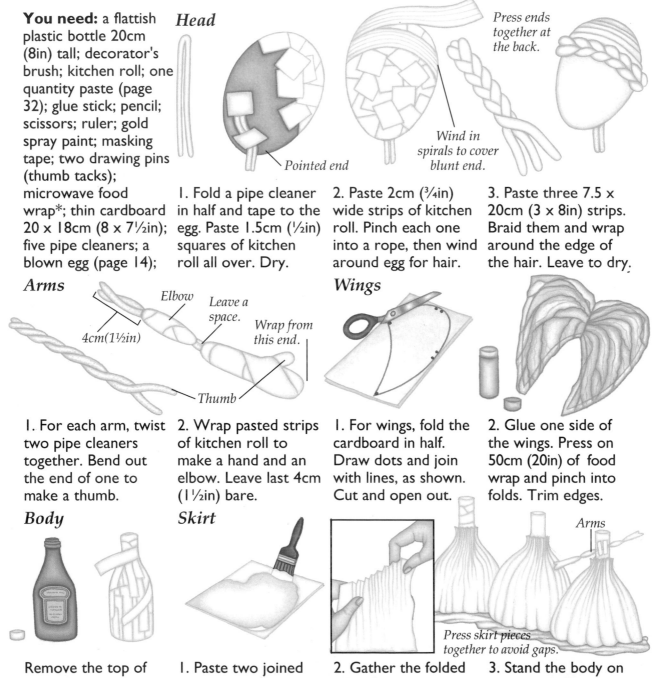

You need: a flattish plastic bottle 20cm (8in) tall; decorator's brush; kitchen roll; one quantity paste (page 32); glue stick; pencil; scissors; ruler; gold spray paint; masking tape; two drawing pins (thumb tacks); microwave food wrap*; thin cardboard 20 x 18cm (8 x 7½in); five pipe cleaners; a blown egg (page 14);

Head

Pointed end

Press ends together at the back.

Wind in spirals to cover blunt end.

1. Fold a pipe cleaner in half and tape to the egg. Paste 1.5cm (½in) squares of kitchen roll all over. Dry.

2. Paste 2cm (¾in) wide strips of kitchen roll. Pinch each one into a rope, then wind around egg for hair.

3. Paste three 7.5 x 20cm (3 x 8in) strips. Braid them and wrap around the edge of the hair. Leave to dry.

Arms

Elbow

Leave a space.

4cm(1½in)

Wrap from this end.

Thumb

1. For each arm, twist two pipe cleaners together. Bend out the end of one to make a thumb.

2. Wrap pasted strips of kitchen roll to make a hand and an elbow. Leave last 4cm (1½in) bare.

Wings

1. For wings, fold the cardboard in half. Draw dots and join with lines, as shown. Cut and open out.

2. Glue one side of the wings. Press on 50cm (20in) of food wrap and pinch into folds. Trim edges.

Body

Remove the top of the plastic bottle. Paste strips of kitchen roll all over the bottle. Leave to dry.

Skirt

Arms

Press skirt pieces together to avoid gaps.

1. Paste two joined pieces of kitchen roll. Fold together along perforation. Paste the top layer again.

2. Gather the folded edge. Press onto the front of the body. Add two more pieces around the body.

3. Stand the body on food wrap. Turn lower edge of skirt under so it balloons out. Dry. Tape arms to the back.

Sleeves

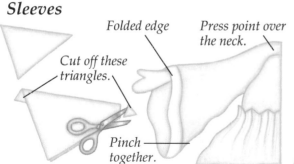

Folded edge

Press point over the neck.

Cut off these triangles.

Pinch together.

1. Paste a 20 x 20cm (8 x 8in) square of kitchen roll. Fold it diagonally. Turn over 1.5cm (½in) at fold.

2. Drape it over one arm. Open out the wide end. Repeat on the other arm.

For her trumpet, or other ideas, see next page

Bodice

1. Paste two joined pieces of kitchen roll. Fold at perforation, then in half. Turn the sides under neatly.

This angel is probably the hardest project in the book, but it makes a beautiful Christmas decoration.

2. Pinch one side into gathers and press onto the waist. Drape the rest over the neck and gather onto the back.

Allow plenty of time for drying at different stages. You may need five or six days to finish it.

THE ANGEL CONTINUES ON THE NEXT PAGE

The sash

1. Paste an 8 x 15cm (3 x 6in) strip of kitchen roll. Pinch it in so it pleats. Wrap around the waist to cover the edges.

2. Trim sash, overlap and press to fasten at the back. Bend arms forward at the elbows and rearrange the sleeves. Leave to dry.

Finishing off

1. Wrap a pasted 2cm (¾in) strip of kitchen roll around the pipe cleaners to pad the neck.

2. Poke a hole in the bottle's neck with a pencil point. Press in the pipe cleaners up to the padding. Dry.

3. Take the angel outside and place the body and the wings on lots of newspaper. Spray gold and dry.

4. Attach the wings to the angel's back with drawing pins (thumb tacks). Add accessories (see right).

26

Other ideas

To make a trumpet, cut an 11cm (4½in) square from white paper. Roll it up, making one end tight. Glue and spray gold.

Make a sheet of music with a folded piece of white paper. Dip it into cold tea to make it look old. Add some music with a black pen.

For a scroll, cut a strip of white paper. Dip in cold tea. Curl by wrapping ends around a pencil in opposite directions.

You could add braid around the neck and brightly painted touches.

Puppets

You need: an apple; a carrot; newspaper; paste (page 32); craft knife; scissors; thin string; hairbrush; paints; two 23cm (9in) green felt squares; scraps of brown and black felt; cardboard; red yarn; big needle; tracing paper; kitchen paper; pencil; two toy eyes; glue stick; two small pebbles; paper clips; sewing pins; clear tape; ruler; two thin 17cm (6in) sticks.

Head

1. Make a papier mâché apple (see pages 4-5). Split open from top to bottom to remove the apple.

String

Felt strip hangs out.

Paint face light brown.

2. Knot one end of 32cm (12½in) of string. Cut a felt strip 2 x 2.5cm (¾ x 1¾in). Glue into one half as shown. Rejoin apple.

3. Crumple and roll a scrap of pasted kitchen paper for a nose. Glue it on. Paste paper strips over it. Paint when dry. Put in eyes (page 21).

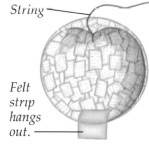

Thread yarn through with a needle and tie here.

Arrange hair around central string.

Brushing makes yarn fuzz out.

4. Cut cardboard 8 x 10cm (3 x 4in). Wind yarn around the long sides. Tie the loops at one edge. Cut loops at the other edge.

5. Hold where the yarn is tied and brush both ends gently. Glue to top of head. Pull fuzz from the brush to glue on as brows and moustache.

You can make this troll puppet stamp his feet angrily.

Slip a small buckle onto his belt before you glue it on (see next page), if you like.

PUPPETS CONTINUE ON THE NEXT PAGE.

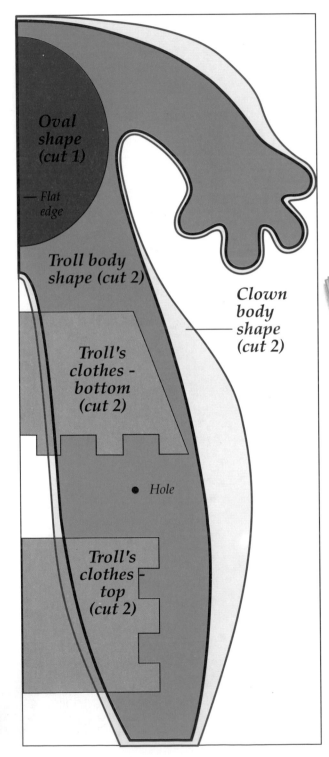

Oval shape (cut 1)

— Flat edge

Troll body shape (cut 2)

Clown body shape (cut 2)

Troll's clothes - bottom (cut 2)

• Hole

Troll's clothes - top (cut 2)

The body

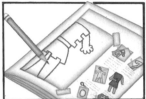

1. Fold the tracing paper. Place the fold along the flat far edge of the troll pattern on the left. Trace the green body shape.

2. Turn tracing over and go over the lines you can see through it (don't forget the dots for holes). Open out to see whole shape.

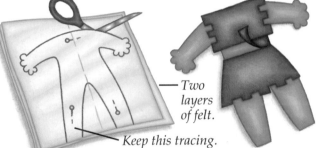

— Two layers of felt.

Keep this tracing.

3. Pin tracing to both green felt squares and cut out. Trace the clothes pieces in the same way. Cut two of each from brown felt.

4. Glue a clothes top and bottom to each body shape. Glue on narrow black felt strips at the waist on both sides as a belt.

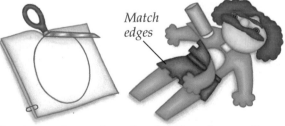

Match edges

5. Trace the red oval pattern on the left in the same way. Attach it to cardboard with paper clips and cut it out.

6. Glue the cardboard oval to the wrong side of one body. Glue the tab from the head to the same piece. Glue on second body piece.

Feet

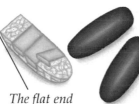

The flat end is the heel.

1. Paste three layers of paper onto 6cm (2½in) of the pointed end of a carrot. Dry. Slice lengthways to remove carrot.

2. Glue a pebble into each heel. Pad the shapes with paper and paste three layers of strips on top as a sole. Dry, then paint black.

Putting together

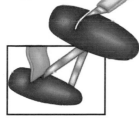

Use a pencil.

1. Cut slits on the shoes 2cm (¾in) from the heel. Glue the ends of the felt legs and push into the slits with a scissor blade.

Pull head upright and tie to middle of stick.

3. Wind leg strings around the stick, 2cm (¾in) from each end. Make both 41cm (16in) long, then tie. Tie the head string on.

2. Replace pattern over troll and poke holes in legs, as marked. Knot one end of two 46cm (18in) pieces of string. Thread through holes.

Clown

To make this clown, follow the same steps as for the troll, only trace the red clown pattern for the body and don't make the troll's clothes. See how to decorate it on the right. Paint the head white with a clown's face.

Jerk the ends of the stick up and down to make the puppet walk.

This hair is yellow yarn, not fuzzed.

Make a cone-shaped hat from felt glued to cardboard. (see angel's trumpet, page 26).

Paint string, if you like.

Sew a running stitch along one long edge of strips of felt and net about 4cm (1¾in) wide. Gather, and sew around the neck for a ruff.

Trace the hands again and cut from white felt. Glue on.

Glue on bright felt shapes, buttons and sequins.

Paint the shoes brightly.

29

Lizard planter

You will need: large newspapers; six egg cartons; masking tape; scissors: plastic or cardboard box about 20 x 15cm (8 x 6in) and 15cm (6in) deep* (box A); plastic or cardboard box about 17cm (7in) square and 9cm (4in) deep** (box B); thin cardboard; felt-tip pen; two-three quantities paper pulp and one of paste (page 32); white emulsion paint; paints; small decorating brush; PVA (household) glue; craft knife; cocktail stick.

The planter takes four or five days to make but is well worth it. You may need help with some steps.

Stem

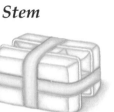

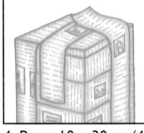

Pull tightly.

1. Tape the egg cartons firmly into three pairs, bumpy sides together. Pile them into a tower and tape it strongly.

2. Lay the tower on a whole open newspaper. Trim paper to fit, roll the tower up in it and tape. Repeat until paper is 1cm (½in) thick.

3. This is the stem. Stand it on cardboard. Draw around it, cut out the shape and tape it to one end of the stem. Stand stem on it.

4. Paste 10 x 30cm (4 x 12in) strips of newspaper around the stem and over the top. Add another layer up and down.

5. When it is dry (a few hours), repeat step 4 twice. That makes six layers in all, drying completely after every two layers.

Top and base

Cut hole slightly bigger than drawn.

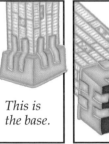

This is the base.

Do layers in alternate directions.

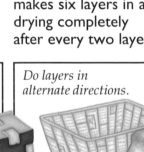

1. Spread glue on the top of the stem, set box A (see list above) centrally on it and add tape to hold very firmly in place.

2. Turn box B (see list above) upside down and stand the tower on it. Draw around it, then cut out the shape.

3. Push the stem into the hole to touch the floor and tape firmly. Draw around the base onto cardboard, cut out and tape on.

4. Cover the boxes with three layers of strips. Dry. Cover the whole planter with a thin layer of pulp. Dry completely (4-5 days).

Paint three layers of varnish (see page 8) inside and line with two layers of silver foil to waterproof. Varnish outside if you want it to be shiny.

Lizard and leaves

Turn pattern over for a lizard going the other way.

Paint black and red striped lizards and greenish-brown leaves.

Copy this lizard, bigger, onto thin cardboard. Do the blue lines first, red next, then green. Cut out. Draw around it onto the stem.

The blue planter is dry-brushed green (see below). Its stem is two egg cartons and its top is a papier mâché bowl.

Add leaf shapes. Build up all the shapes with pulp. Mark leaves with a cocktail stick. When completely dry, paint white emulsion all over.

Paint inside too.

Paint it yellow. Put orange on the brush, wipe most of it off on paper, then brush over the yellow. This is called dry-brushing.

The red planter is just two boxes back to back.

31

Recipes

Paste recipe

This recipe makes about 1½ cups of paste. If you want a different amount, use 1 part of flour to 3 parts of water. Use a little extra water for runny paste. Ask for help to use the stove.

You will need:
whisk; cup; flour; bowl; saucepan; wooden spoon.

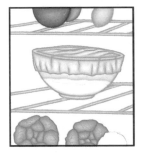

Don't overcook the mixture as it will become too thick.

1. In a bowl, whisk a cup of flour with a cup of water. Add two more cups of water and mix well to get rid of any lumps.

2. Put the mixture into a saucepan and bring it to the boil, stirring constantly. Allow to cool completely.

3. To store, cover tightly with plastic food wrap and keep it in a refrigerator. It will last for several days.

You can use two parts PVA (household) glue and one part water or buy non-toxic paste from toy or craft stores instead. Don't use wallpaper paste as it contains toxic fungicides.

Papier mâché pulp

This is one quantity of pulp. You will be told if you need more.

You will need:
blender (optional); newspaper; large bowl; one tablespoon PVA (household) glue mixed with one tablespoon paste (see above); a mug; a sieve.

This pulp is made with glue and paste. Paste-only pulp is not as strong. Glue-only pulp is harder to model. For extra-strong pulp add fillers - sawdust (from pet shops) or decorators' filler.

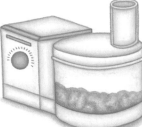

1. Cut or tear several layers of newpaper into 1.5cm (½in) squares. Pack lightly into a mug to fill it.

2. **Either:** put the paper into a blender. Cover it with water and blend with lots of short bursts.

Or: Soak the paper in hot water for 3 hours. Then knead with your fingers to make a pulp.

Tips

If stored pulp gets too wet, squeeze it out and add glue.

Always protect work areas with lots of old newspapers.

Keep a damp rag handy for cleaning up.

3. Squeeze water from the pulp in a sieve. Put the pulp into the bowl. Add a tablespoon of glue/paste mix.

4. Knead it together well. Add more glue mix until it feels like squashy clay. Store in a bag in a refrigerator.